ST. JEROME AND THE LION

ST. JEROME
AND THE
LION

by

Rumer Godden

DRAWINGS BY
· JEAN PRIMROSE ·

NEW YORK

THE VIKING PRESS

Library of Congress catalog card number: 61-13669

St. Jerome and the Lion appeared with different
illustrations in the *Ladies' Home Journal*

I must thank Mr. Maurice FitzGerald for
making me a translation from the *Late Latin*
of Vita Divi Hieronymi (Migne, P. L. XXII.
c. 209 ff.) on which this poem is based, but
must also make acknowledgement to Miss
Helen Waddell for two particularly vivid
phrases in her translation in *Beasts and Saints:*
for 'The brothers scattered like swallows', and
for the lion's 'affable' rumbling.

R.G.

LITHOGRAPHED IN THE U.S.A. BY AFFILIATED LITHOGRAPHERS

ST. JEROME
AND THE
LION

by

Rumer Godden

DRAWINGS BY
· JEAN PRIMROSE ·

NEW YORK

THE VIKING PRESS

Library of Congress catalog card number: 61-13669

St. Jerome and the Lion appeared with different
illustrations in the *Ladies' Home Journal*

I must thank Mr. Maurice FitzGerald for
making me a translation from the *Late Latin*
of Vita Divi Hieronymi (Migne, P. L. XXII.
c. 209 ff.) on which this poem is based, but
must also make acknowledgement to Miss
Helen Waddell for two particularly vivid
phrases in her translation in *Beasts and Saints :*
for 'The brothers scattered like swallows', and
for the lion's 'affable' rumbling.

R.G.

LITHOGRAPHED IN THE U.S.A. BY AFFILIATED LITHOGRAPHERS

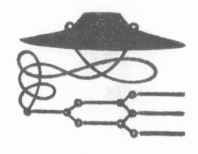

For May Massee

I

To Bethlehem, with its white stone and towers,
　　its brown hills where larks sing, and its unexpected
　　flowers:
iris, anemones, scillas and cyclamen,
that scatter the bare gullies; to Bethlehem
where Christ was born, came the great Saint, Jerome,
with his red hat[1] and his Bible, seeking, from the stir and dust
　　of Rome,
peace for holiness and study, and built a convent[2] on a hill
　　to be his home.

---

[1] Though St Jerome was not a Cardinal – there were no Cardinals then – he is always
shown in paintings with a Cardinal's hat so that I, too, have given him one.

[2] In Italy the religious orders have some things the other way round from us. Monks
live in convents, nuns in monasteries.

With him came brother monks, some wise in books,
some farmed, wheat, vines, olives: some were gardeners, cooks,
or wove wool for the monks' habits, or cured leather
for their sandals; but all together
kept the strict rule: 'We work to live and live to pray.'
Even the hens were trained to lay
eggs clean enough for angels, while at break of day

the cocks did duty, crowing three times to wake
the brothers. The ass was panniered and, though naughty,
      learned to make
useful journeys: oxen plodded, turning the wheel
to mill the grain: the lambs gave their fleece wool:
even the fish were caught for Fridays: none was idle
and, burning his light, all night, Jerome kept vigil[1]
as into the people's Latin he transcribed the Bible.

---

[1] It is to Jerome that we owe the 'Vulgate', the first 'people's' Bible, completed in 405.

ONE February, there came an afternoon
          when the hill villages and fields around the convent
          shone
painted with light. Each cypress threw its shadow; the clear
young blue of the sky was shrill with larks. In this springtime
     of the year
the brothers took their recreation out of doors
(they needed recreation just as you need yours)
in the long day of work and prayer, an hour's welcome pause.

They walked down the lane, chattering at their ease
and watching the wind blow green and silver in the olive trees,
when all at once there came a dreadsome sound
that broke the air and shook the ground,
rolling from hill to hill; it seemed to hem
the world in thunder and, onto that quiet path that led
     to Bethlehem,
a great maned lion stepped, not twenty yards from them.

Prrt! The brothers scattered like swallows: their cries came
back on the wind as they ran, calling sweet Mary's name
to save them. Nor did one wait
to help another but, pell-mell, in at the gate
they tumbled, and slammed it fast with bolt and lock.
Saint Jerome was left outside; unmoved as a rock
he stayed as a good shepherd stays who has to guard his flock.

OD be with me,' he prayed, but still the lion came on,
roaring to split the sky, but now his tone
seemed to the Saint more hurt than angry; and then
he saw
this lion limped on three legs, one front paw
hung swollen, bleeding, and misery
had so furrowed his face that the Saint could see
he had not come to devour but to ask for charity.

For three nights and days the lion had not slept.
His flanks were thin, his gold eyes wept
as he wandered in pain and fever, roaring, as if asking why
a lion should suffer. 'A weasel or goat or bad serpent, but I,
the King of Beasts, to find a thorn such woe!'
(He had fallen into a thicket of thorns a week ago
and one had festered.) All this Saint Jerome seemed to know,

and laid his hand on the hot snuff-coloured brow.
'Lord Jesus is the King of Kings,' he said, 'but I shall read
     you how
He suffered with a hundred thorn wreath pricks.'
The lion listened thoughtfully, gave the hand lion licks
to show his pity, and tried to sink his roaring to a moan.
'Lord Jesus! Then His beast is not alone,'
and he limped up to the convent gate with Saint Jerome.

THEY knocked,
and smiled at one another now to find it locked.
The brothers opened trembling, but when they saw Jerome come
walking in with the lion, they were dumb
with amazement — and shame at leaving their master outside.
'Punish us,' they implored him, but Jerome only cried,
'Bring herbs, hot water, linen.' Then, with as much fuss, as if
a pride

of lions were wounded, they set about
bathing the paw. First they pulled the long thorn out.
The operation was painful, the lion could not help a howl,
which, looking up into Jerome's face, he hastily sank to a growl,
and, as pus streamed out, to a whimper;
then, when the paw was poulticed and dressed, came a sound
that made a stir
through the whole convent: a contented happy rumbling
that was the lion's purr.

A GENTLE time passed that helped to heal the paw.
The lion was given a cell with a bed of the
cleanest straw,
and kept the convent hours and shared the convent food.
When the brothers sang in choir or said their Mass, he stood
quiet outside the chapel door, or else he lay
with his front paws put together, as if to say,
'I am a Christian lion now and I too can pray.'

But a day came that made the heart of every brother grieve.
The paw was healed and the lion was well enough to leave;
so they blessed him and set him free, opening the convent gate,
but he did not go but flattened himself at Saint Jerome's feet
and wagged his tail.[1] When they tried to make him move
he growled under his breath but, at once to show his love,
patted the Saint with a paw made soft as a velvet glove.

[1] I do not think lions wag their tails when they want to please, rather the reverse, but
the legend says this one did, so I have let him.

Now for a solemn conclave, Jerome put on his
red hat, and round him in the choir,[1] the other
brothers sat.
'That we admit the lion,' said one of the monks, 'I move,'
but a crabbed old monk got up and said, 'I don't approve.
A lion is always a lion. This is a wild beast still,
not to be trusted with lambs or chickens, for he has to make
his kill.'
'I trust him,' said Saint Jerome and the lion thumped his tail.

---

[1] In small convents in the old days, business seems to have been done in the choir.

He was admitted, but now there arose a new
problem: what work could the lion do?
If he lived in the convent, he must keep the convent rule,
but lions cannot lay eggs, or be ridden, or sheared for wool.
For two days the brothers debated, but the lion was quite content
to attend on Saint Jerome wherever he came and went
(artists have always painted him in every picture of the Saint).

At last the youngest brother came, hands in his sleeves, to ask
permission to speak: 'We are short-handed, yet it is still my task
to take the ass each day to pasture,
watching over her there, for you know ass nature
is wilful indeed. Then to fetch firewood we go on
to the woodsman. If the lion could guard her, my task is gone.'
'But would he agree?' asked the Saint and stopped, for an affable
        rumbling came from the lion.

SUMMER and autumn and winter and spring,
    after Mass had been said, each pleasant morning
      the ass went to graze, most modestly
for she respected the lion's eye
(he had only to rumble and bristle his whiskers),
and, though there were still those baneful whispers,
he trotted her back in time for Vespers

with her panniers full;
and, after taking his evening meal
(waiting first for Grace), he stretched himself
    by Jerome's table
and, sometimes all night, they conned the Bible.[1]
'Our lion,' praised the brothers, 'has grown so mild
he could truly be led by a little child.'
'He's a beast,' said the crabbed old monk. 'A beast and wild.'

[1] There is a painting of them doing this in the National Gallery, London.

IT was high summer; the hazy noonday's tropical
    heat lay on the land, and the ass's lazy rhythmical
    cropping, close by his nose,
as the lion kept guard made his eyelids close
(he had been up all night). Forty winks, then he opened an eye
but the little she-ass was still close by,
and he fell asleep stertorously.

Up went her heels and off the ass ran
to tread down the crops, while stuffing her mouth, till a caravan
with bells that gonged came along the road:
merchants and drivers, dark-faced, white robed
and camels with trappings, their harness inlaid
with scarlet; the line of their great humped shadows swayed
beside them. They were going down to Egypt to trade

carpets for oil, and when they saw the ass wandering loose
in the fields, they caught her with a rope and noose.
'Though we must buy hay and corn for her feed,
a quick little ass will be useful to lead
our slow-stepping camels.' The ass did not even nicker or bray
(she liked that talk of corn and hay).
Soon even their dust had dwindled away.

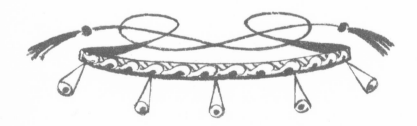

OXEN stabled, lambs in fold, every chicken in its coop.
Benediction was over and, with the smell of incense
and candles, onion soup
filled the convent, fragrantly,
and in the long refectory
a napkin, bowl and barley loaf showed where each brother
was to sit.
The little bronze oil lamps were lit
and shone like fireflies; but still the brothers stayed, to flit

like brown-robed shadows, up and down; seeking, crying,
round the gate.
The empty stall, the lion's untouched plate
made sad forebodings. The old monk gloated: 'Imp of sin!'
(he meant the lion). 'Let us go in
and have our supper.' Jerome would not break a crust
without his friend. Again he said, 'I trust
the lion.' Then late, late, in the dust

they saw a figure, desperate, prone,
as carved by grief as if in stone;
it was the lion — and alone.

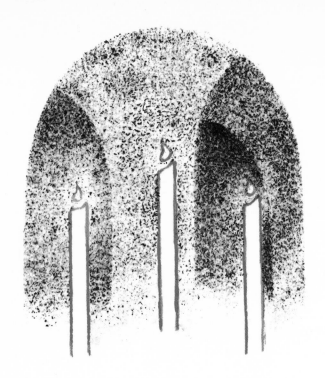

II

'WHERE is the ass?' The brothers flocked
round the gateway, angry and shocked.
'Where is the ass?' but beasts are dumb
nor could the lion weep, his eyes were numb
with his first fault; and the old monk chortled: 'You see,
    your good
Christian lion despised our food
and has eaten the ass. I said he would.'

OXEN stabled, lambs in fold, every chicken in its coop.
Benediction was over and, with the smell of incense
and candles, onion soup
filled the convent, fragrantly,
and in the long refectory
a napkin, bowl and barley loaf showed where each brother
was to sit.
The little bronze oil lamps were lit
and shone like fireflies; but still the brothers stayed, to flit

like brown-robed shadows, up and down; seeking, crying,
round the gate.
The empty stall, the lion's untouched plate
made sad forebodings. The old monk gloated: 'Imp of sin!'
(he meant the lion). 'Let us go in
and have our supper.' Jerome would not break a crust
without his friend. Again he said, 'I trust
the lion.' Then late, late, in the dust

they saw a figure, desperate, prone,
as carved by grief as if in stone;
it was the lion — and alone.

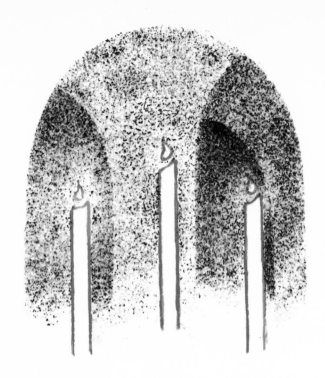

II

'WHERE is the ass?' The brothers flocked
round the gateway, angry and shocked.
'Where is the ass?' but beasts are dumb
nor could the lion weep, his eyes were numb
with his first fault; and the old monk chortled: 'You see,
your good
Christian lion despised our food
and has eaten the ass. I said he would.'

With sticks and stones they pelted to drive the lion outside.
'Away with you,' 'Hard of heart,' 'Glutton,' 'Thief,' they cried.
'You can fill your greedy belly for yourself, you sinner,'
and 'Who took our pretty ass to eat for dinner?'
'Go. Finish her off before the vultures rob
you, as you have robbed us,' until with a howl (a lion's sob),
he ran to Jerome and hid his face in the Saint's robe.

'Gently, my brothers,' said Jerome. 'Consider: are these ways
    meant
to touch the heart of one who has sinned and make him penitent?
No. Treat him, I ask, as before and let him still be fed,
and do not nag at him and make him wretched.
Only' — and here the Saint spoke gravely and to the lion's face —
'as through him we have suffered and lost our little ass,
the lion must be our servant, exactly as she was.'

A king to wear harness! Be domestic! The very stones
    would laugh
to see a lion carrying faggots home along a public path.
'I will not,' growled the lion and rumbled dangerously
    under his breath.
'With a few strokes of this paw I could mangle you all to death.'
From the Saint's stern eye, it seemed that a dart
of light struck the lion. 'For the strong to be strong is easy,
    but there is a better part:
for the strong to submit and be gentle is perfect of heart;

the pattern is our Lord Jesus.' This without a word being said,
and the lion gave a sigh — it rent him like a tornado — and bowed
    his head.

FOR a beast to school himself is hard, the lion grew thin;
    his claws would often come out though he fought
    to keep them in;
and often he bristled with anger, for to make him feel his disgrace,
when the brothers chanced to meet him, each would
    turn away his face;
and when he came to the chapel, they shooed him from his place.

He was denied his cell and slept in the ass's stall.

His golden body, not used to harness, had so many a rub and gall

that he was ashamed to appear in the study, and lay out in the
    corridor,

wakeful, for he had lost an animals' innocent snore;

but his mane shone like a halo and slowly he grew so meek

that when the brothers rebuffed him, he turned the other
    velvet cheek.

Yet still his penance dragged on for week after weary week.

O NE evening as he trotted home — he had learned to trot
with his faggots — as if prompted he came to a sudden
    stop

and turned aside to where the lane joined
    the Damascus-Egypt road

and waited there, not knowing why, until a dust cloud showed

coming nearer. His ears pricked. Excitement rippled

under his skin. His whiskers twitched. His tail tuft trembled,

and deep in his throat a warning rumbled.

Soon, in the dust, he saw men, dark-faced, white robed;
    and, strung
one behind the other, camels. Trappings and harness swung
and the bell notes gonged. It was a caravan come
up, rich, laden from Egypt and travelling home.
The lion looked nearer, his gold eyes grew astonished
    and his heart began to swell
with royal anger, for there, in front of the camels,
    in bridle and tinkling bell,
finicked and dawdled a little she-ass that he knew very well.

Up to heaven went his furious roar.

His harness splintered, faggots were scattered, as he bore

down on the caravan. Men fled to the fields. The camels
    plunged after the men,

but the lion was a skilful drover now and he rounded
    them up again.

One quick growl at the ass and she became nimble, sedate

and, as if she had never been away, led the camels straight

off the road, up the lane and the lion drove them all in
    at the convent gate.

He raced to find Saint Jerome, tugging at his gown,
and, in and out of corridors, chased the brothers up and down,
pushing, pulling. 'The devil is in him,' they cried. 'Fetch
    the bell and Book.'[1]
'Not the devil,' said Jerome, 'his good angel. Look
how we are brought to justice.' In a minute, every soul
had gathered in the courtyard, where the lion, in full control,
made the milling camels kneel to show the she-ass untouched,
    alive and whole.

[1] When a priest is asked to curse anyone he does it solemnly with a candle, a bell, and a Bible.

The monks knelt too, asking his pardon and, no longer sad
    and melancholic,
the lion patted them to stand upright. Then began to bound
    and frolic
through the convent, flattening himself before each brother,
wagging his tail as if to say, 'We forgive each other.'
As each blessed him, he bounded up to race
back to Saint Jerome, then to the ass, back to the Saint. It was
    pure joy, no trace
of righteous pride except — when he met the old monk, it was
    the lion who turned away his face.

A brother aired the lion's cell, strewing sweet herbs
    to make his bed.
Others swept his place by the chapel and put down a carpet
    of cardinal red.

The brother cooks in the kitchen took counsel
    of what he liked to eat
and asked leave, though it was Friday, to brim
    his plate with meat.
When the day was over and shadows filled the evening sky,
the lion came into the study and, where he used to lie,
stretched himself by the table with a contented sigh.
'He is purring,' whispered the brothers and tiptoed saying,
    'Glory to God on high.'

III

W HAT of the camels? Late that night a timid knocking
was heard
and the merchants stood outside, too ashamed
to speak a word;
but the brothers had learned a lesson: they let the merchants in
and gave them back their camels; nor did anyone mention the sin
of stealing away the ass. 'From this day,' said the wiser brothers,
'We shall let God sift
good and evil.' Then from their Egyptian cruses, the merchants
made such a gift
that would keep the convent in oil for a year (used with
convent thrift).

'And we shall bring more,' they said, 'next year, as we pass by on
our camels; but, first, please, you must tie up your lion.'

IN Bethlehem, with its white stone and towers,
this story blossomed long ago; and, as flowers
are pressed to keep before they fade,
a scholar wrote it in old Latin, and made
it into a book. The brothers are quiet now. No convent
stands upon the hill.

Jerome is with the Saints, and I am sure that,
by God's will,
though the hat and the Bible were left behind,
the lion is with him still.

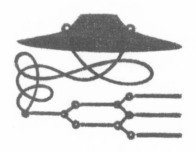